THE PICTURE OF DORIAN GRAY

THE PICTURE OF DORIAN GRAY

Oscar Wilde

An imprint of Om Books International

Reprinted in 2017

Om
K[DZ

An imprint of Om Books International

Corporate & Editorial Office
A-12, Sector 64, Noida 201 301
Uttar Pradesh, India
Phone: +91 120 477 4100
Email: editorial@ombooks.com
Website: www.ombooksinternational.com

Sales Office
107, Ansari Road, Darya Ganj
New Delhi 110 002, India
Phone: +91 11 4000 9000
Fax: +91 11 2327 8091
Email: sales@ombooks.com
Website: www.ombooks.com

© Om Books International 2015

Adapted by Subhojit Sanyal

ISBN: 9789384225360

Printed in India

10 9 8 7 6 5 4 3

Contents

1.	The Portrait	7
2.	Dorian Gray	31
3.	Enquiry	57
4.	Love	65
5.	Sibyl Vane	83
6.	The Engagement	95
7.	The Play	103
8.	Death	119
9.	A Change	127
10.	The Schoolroom	135
11.	The Mystery	143
12.	Train to Paris	151
13.	Murder	159
14.	Alan Campbell	169
15.	Evidence Removed	181
16.	James Meets Dorian	189
17.	He's Back	199
18.	The Stable	205
19.	Redemption	215
20.	The Ugly Portrait	225
	About the Author	236
	Characters	237
	Questions	238

Chapter One

The Portrait

It was a perfect summer day. The studio was bathed in fresh sunlight. A soft breeze blew in through the window, carrying the rich fragrance of roses and lilacs from the garden outside. The noise of the crowded London city did not reach them. The only sound that broke the silence outside the studio window was of the bees buzzing on the flowers in the garden.

The studio had two occupants, the artist Basil Hallward and his friend Lord Henry Wotton.

At the centre of the room, on the artist's easel, stood the full-length portrait of an extraordinarily handsome man. The artist stood looking at the

7

painting intently. He smiled at the painting, pleased with the work, then closed his eyes and placed his fingers on the lid, as if trying to remember something.

"It is your best work Basil," said his friend Lord Henry, who was sitting on a divan closeby.

When Basil continued to stare at the portrait, Lord Henry added, "You should display it at the Grosvernor next year. I would have recommended the Academy, but it is too crowded. It either has too many people or too many paintings, and I don't know which one is worse. The Grosvernor is really the only place."

"I won't send it anywhere," said Basil, taking his friend by surprise.

"And why not?" asked Lord Henry in astonishment. He added, "You artists are strange people. You want to be recognised, but you will not seize the opportunity. The only thing worse than being talked about is not being talked about. This portrait will make a place for you above all other young and old artists."

Basil did not immediately respond to Lord Henry's question. He seemed to be in a dilemma, about whether he should reveal the real reason.

"I know you will laugh, but I cannot show it in public. I have put too much of myself in this portrait," Basil responded finally, and Lord Henry laughed.

"Basil, I didn't know you were so vain. But I really don't see any resemblance between you and the young Adonis, with a handsome face and perfect features staring at us from the portrait. Beauty, real beauty, ends where an intellectual expression begins. Intellect is in itself a mode of exaggeration, and destroys the harmony of any face. The moment one sits down to think, one becomes all nose, or all forehead, or something horrid. Don't flatter yourself, Basil. You are not in the least like him," said Lord Henry when he had stopped laughing.

"Of course I am not like him. It is sad but perfection like this is bound to bring unhappiness. There is a fatality about all physical and intellectual distinction. It is better not to be different from one's fellows. The ugly and the stupid have the best of it in this world. They can sit at their ease and gape at the play. If they know nothing of victory, they are at least spared the knowledge of defeat. They live as we all should live — undisturbed, indifferent and without disquiet. They neither bring ruin upon others, nor ever receive it from alien hands. People like you or me too are bound to see much sadness because of what we have in abundance — you for your wealth and status, and me for my art. Dorian Gray with his perfect looks will also not escape this fate," said Basil, with a faraway look in his eyes.

"Dorian Gray, is that his name?" asked Lord Henry, as he walked across the studio to stand in front of the portrait.

"Yes, but I did not want to tell you this," said Basil ambiguously before adding, "When I like somebody a lot, I do not tell their names to anyone. I feel that by revealing the name,

I am surrendering a part of that friendship to the others. I have grown to love secrecy. It seems to bring a great deal of romance into one's life. Do you think it's foolish of me?"

"This is all right. I understand secrecy as well as any married man, though I must admit that my wife is better at hiding things from me. And even though she has caught my lie during our occassional evenings out, she laughs it off," said Lord Henry, similing and smoking his cigar.

"The way you represent marriage is atrocious, but I believe you are a good husband. Your cyniciam is just a pose," said Basil.

"Being natural is a pose, and the most irritating one at that," said Lord Henry, as they both started walking towards the garden and stopped near a wooden bench.

"But now I want you to tell me the real reason why you will not exhibit Dorian Gray's portrait," asked Lord Henry seriously.

After some hesitation, Basil revealed, "Every portrait that is painted by an artist is a reflection

of the artist. The subject of the portrait is only secondary. It is not the subject who is revealed in the painting. It is the one who has coloured the canvas. The reason I don't want to exhibit Dorian Gray's picture is this. I feel it shows the secret of my soul."

Lord Henry laughed at this so-called reason and urged his friend to explain further.

Basil Hallward then told him how he had met Dorian Gray. He said, "Two months ago, I accepted an invitation to Lady Brandon's house. Poor artists like us have to show our faces to the society to prove that we are not savages. You once told me that with an evening coat and tie, one can gain a reputation of a gentleman. I had been in the party for around ten minutes talking to someone when I became aware of somebody watching me. I turned half-way round and saw Dorian Gray for the first time. When our eyes met, I felt that I was growing pale with fear. I knew that I had come face-to-face with someone of fascinating personality, who may absorb my

whole nature, my whole soul, my very art itself. I did not want any external influence in my life. You know, Harry, how independent I am by nature. I have always been my own master, had at least always been so, till I met Dorian Gray. Then — but I don't know how to explain it to you — something seemed to tell me that I was on the verge of a terrible crisis in my life. I had a strange feeling that fate had in store for me exquisite joys and exquisite sorrows. I turned to leave the room. It was not conscience that made me do so, it was a sort of cowardice. I take no credit to myself for trying to escape."

"Conscience and cowardice are really the same things, Basil. Conscience is the trade-name of the firm. That is all," explained Lord Henry.

"I don't believe that, Harry, and I don't believe you do either. My motive may have been pride, for I used to be very proud; I certainly struggled to the door. There, of course, I stumbled against Lady Brandon. 'You are not going to run away

so soon, Mr Hallward?' she screamed out. You know her curiously shrill voice?"

"Yes; she is a peacock in everything but beauty," said Lord Henry, pulling the daisy to bits with his long nervous fingers.

"I could not get rid of her. She introduced me to royalties, and people with stars and garters, and elderly ladies with gigantic tiaras and parrot noses, as if I was her dearest friend. I had only met her once before, but she took it into her head to lionise me. I believe some picture of mine had made a great success at the time, at least had been chattered about in the penny newspapers, which is the nineteenth-century standard of immortality. Suddenly I found myself face-to-face with the young man whose personality had so strangely stirred me. Our eyes met again and I asked Lady Brandon to introduce me to him. It was simply inevitable. We would have spoken to each other without any introduction. I am sure of that. Dorian told me so afterwards. He, too, felt that we were destined to know each other."

"And how did Lady Brandon describe this wonderful young man?" asked his companion. "Lady Brandon treats her guests exactly as an auctioneer treats his goods. She either explains them entirely away or tells one everything about them except what one wants to know."

"Poor Lady Brandon! You are hard on her, Harry! But what did she say about Dorian Gray?" said Hallward listlessly.

"Oh, something like, 'Charming boy, poor dear mother and I absolutely inseparable. Quite forget what he does ... afraid he ... doesn't do anything ... oh, yes, plays the piano ... or is it the violin, dear Mr Gray?' Neither of us could help laughing, and we became friends at once."

"Laughter is not at all a bad beginning for a friendship, and it is by far the best ending for one," said the young lord, plucking another daisy.

Hallward shook his head. "You don't understand what friendship is, Harry," he murmured, "or what enmity is, for that matter.

You like everyone; that is to say, you are indifferent to every one."

"How horribly unjust of you!" cried Lord Henry, but not looking offended at all. "I choose my friends for their good looks, my acquaintances for their good characters and my enemies for their good intellects. I have not got one who is a fool. They are all men of some intellectual power, and consequently they all appreciate me. Is that very vain of me? I think it is rather vain."

Basil replied, "Well, according to your description, I seem to fall under the category of acquaintance."

Lord Henry said, "No, you are like my friend. I am quite tired of the people of my class and the hypocrisy of the society. But I am not here to discuss the society and it's ways with you. Please tell me more about this Dorian Gray. How often do you meet?"

Basil replied, "I meet him practically every day. It has become necessary for me. My art was important to me, but he is all my art to me now.

I know that his portrait is my best work till now, but he is just more than a model for me. How do I explain this to you? But in some curious way, his personality has suggested to me an entirely new manner in art, an entirely new mode of style. I see things differently, I think of them differently. I can now recreate life in a way that was hidden from me before. 'A dream of form in days of thought' — who is it who says that? I forget; but it is what Dorian Gray has been to me. Do you remember the landscape I painted for which I was offered a huge price? Do you know why I did not want to sell it? It is because Dorian Gray was sitting next to me when I had painted it. His presence made the painting special for me."

"This is extraordinary, Basil. I must meet Dorian Gray," said Lord Henry eagerly.

"You might not find anything special in him," said Basil in response to his friend's excitement.

"If he is not so special, why won't you exhibit his picture?" asked his friend.

"This is because, unintentionally, I have added my curious artistic idolatry for him in this painting. He does not know it, and he will never know it. But the world might guess the nature of my feelings. And I do not want my feelings to be examined under a microscope by the whole world," said Basil.

"But tales of broken heart sell very well."

"But I detest such things. Creation should inspire happiness in the world."

"Does Dorian Gray like you?"

"I am sure that he is fond of me. We do talk about endless things, but sometimes his thoughts and words really hurt me. I realise at those moments that I have given my heart to someone, who takes me for granted."

"But you may tire of him one day, like he may tire of you. One day, you will look at him with adoration and the next you will silently reproach him for his flaws. Then, you will get hurt by something he said, and the next time he calls you, you will be cold and distant to him. The worst part

of having a romance of any kind is that it leaves one so unromantic."

"As long as I live, Dorian Gray's personality will continue to influence me," said Basil emphatically.

"Oh! I just remembered where I have heard Dorian Gray's name. My aunt, Lady Agatha, had mentioned a young man who would be helping her in the East End."

"I don't want you to meet him," said Basil suddenly.

"And why not?" asked his friend.

Before Basil could respond, his butler arrived. He announced that Dorian Gray had come. Lord Henry laughed and said, "Now you will have to introduce me to Dorian Gray."

Basil told Lord Henry, solemnly, "Don't spoil him. Your influence could be bad."

"What nonsense are you saying," responded his friend with a smile. The two then walked on to meet the subject of their long discussion.

Chapter Two

Dorian Gray

Dorian Gray was sitting at the piano. His back was towards the door and only he heard the footsteps behind him. So he did not see Lord Henry and Basil enter the room.

"You must lend me these Basil. I want to learn them," he said picking up a couple of pages of a musical piece.

"Well, that would depend on how well you sit for the portrait," responded Basil.

"I am tired of sitting. I don't want a life-sized portrait," said Dorian grumpily as he swung on his seat to face them. "Oh, you didn't tell me you had company."

"This is Lord Henry Wotton, Dorian, an old Oxford friend of mine. I was just telling Lord Henry what a great subject you are. But you just spoiled the good impression," said Basil as he introduced the two men.

"You have not spoiled the impression at all Mr Gray. I believe you are my aunt, Lady Agatha's, favourite person," said Lord Henry, shaking hands with Dorian.

"But, I think she hates me now. You see, I forgot about an engagement I had with her, where I was suppose to play duet on the piano with her," said Dorian. "When Aunt Agatha sits on the piano, she makes enough noise for two people," joked Lord Henry, causing Dorian to break into laughter.

As Dorian Gray laughed, Lord Henry observed him. Yes, he was certainly handsome, with his finely curved scarlet lips, his frank blue eyes, his crisp gold hair. There was something in his face that made one trust him at once. All the candour of youth was there, as well as all youth's passionate purity. One felt that he had kept himself unspotted from the world. No wonder Basil Hallward worshipped him.

Basil interrupted his thoughts suddenly by saying, "Henry, I want to finish this portrait today. Hope you will not consider me rude, if I ask you to leave now."

Lord Henry looked at Dorian Gray and asked, "Should I leave, Mr Gray?"

"Oh, please, don't go, Lord Henry. I can see that Basil is in one of his bad moods. You and I can chat," said Dorian emphatically.

Lord Henry asked the artist, "I am sure that you will not mind. You have often told me that you like it when your subjects are relaxed and have someone to chat with."

Basil was not happy with the situation but replied, "If Dorian wishes it, of course, you must stay. Dorian's whims are laws to everybody, except himself."

Lord Henry announced that he was expecting a guest at home and therefore had to leave. He asked Dorian to visit him at his residence on

Curzon street. Dorian jumped up and exclaimed, "Basil, if Lord Henry leaves now, I will leave with him. You never talk when you are painting. It is really dull standing on the platform and trying to look pleasant. Ask Lord Henry to stay. In fact, I insist that he stays."

"Stay, Harry, to oblige Dorian, and to oblige me. Now Dorian, please get up on the platform. Don't move too much. And don't pay much attention to Lord Henry. He is a bad influence on all his friends. I am an exception, of course," Basil said in good humour.

Dorian Gray was quite fascinated with Lord Henry. The latter's playful nature was quite the opposite of his quieter friend Basil.

"Are you really a bad influence?" he asked naively.

Lord Henry was quite amused by Dorian's innocence.

"There is no such thing as good influence. All influence is wrong. This is because to influence another person is to stop him from living his

natural life. His thoughts and behaviour are then not his own. They are just reflections of the person who is influencing him. The real purpose of life is to live one's true nature. Most of us are either afraid of the society or our religion. These two factors influence every aspect of our lives. We are afraid to live our life completely. The only way to be happy is to give expression to all your desires."

Basil, who was painting Dorian Gray, noticed the change on the young man's face as he heard Lord Henry with rapt attention.

Lord Henry, in the meanwhile, continued to talk to Dorian Gray.

"But each of us is afraid to give in to our impulses. But these impulses do not just disappear. They continue to dominate our lives. We keep thinking about them. Therefore, the best thing to do is to give in to your impulses," Lord Henry said ambiguously before adding, "I am sure that you have also experienced thoughts and feelings that have frightened you. They have surely

dominated your daydreams and your dreams in general."

Lord Henry had barely said the last words when an agitated Dorian Gray interrupted him, "Stop. I don't have an answer to this. But there must be an answer. I have to think, or rather not think at all."

For the next few minutes there was absolute silence in the studio. There was a strange brightness in Dorian Gray's eyes, and lips parted with admiration as he stood still, thinking. He admitted to himself that Lord Henry's words had touched a deep chord within him. They had reminded him of something — things that he had not understood since he was a boy. Suddenly, Dorian felt an excitement that he had never experienced before.

Lord Henry stood silently, watching the changing expressions on Dorian's face and was quite amused.

Dorian suddenly announced, "Basil, I am tired of standing. I would like to go to the garden."

Lord Henry added, "And I would very well like to have a cool drink, preferably something with strawberries in it." Basil said, "Certainly, Harry. Please ring the bell before you step out, and when Parker comes, I'll let him know what you need. I have got to work up this background, so I will join you later on. Don't keep Dorian too long. I have never been in better form for painting than I am today. This is going to be my masterpiece. It is my masterpiece as it stands."

As the two sat outside, Lord Henry said, "Let us go and sit in the shade. Parker has brought out the drinks, and if you stay any longer in this glare, you will be quite spoiled, and Basil will never paint you again. You really must not allow yourself to become sunburnt. It would be unbecoming." Dorian was quite bemused with this remark.

"No, you don't feel it now. Some day, when you are old and wrinkled and ugly, when thought has seared your forehead with its lines, and passion branded your lips with its hideous

fires, you will feel it, you will feel it terribly. Yes, Mr Gray, the gods have been good to you. But what the gods give they quickly take away. You have only a few years in which to live really, perfectly and fully. When your youth goes, your beauty will go with it, and then you will suddenly discover that there are no triumphs left for you, or have to content yourself with those mean triumphs that the memory of your past will make more bitter than defeats. The moment I met you I saw that you were quite unconscious of what you really are, of what you really might be. There was so much in you that charmed me that I felt I must tell you something about yourself. I thought how tragic it would be if you were wasted. Youth! Youth! There is absolutely nothing in the world but youth," Lord Henry said with a strange note in his voice. Dorian listened to him with rapt attention, absorbing each word.

The strange atmosphere that Lord Henry created with his words finally broke as Basil

called out, "Do come in. The light is quite perfect, and you can bring your drinks," to them.

As the two walked into the studio, Lord Henry asked Dorian, "Aren't you glad you met me, Mr Gray?"

"I am. But will I always be glad..." replied Dorian.

"Always! That is a dreadful word. It makes me shudder when I hear it. Women are so fond of using it. They spoil every romance by trying to make it last forever. It is a meaningless word, too. The only difference between a caprice and a lifelong passion is that the caprice lasts a little longer," said Henry.

As they entered the studio, Dorian put his hand upon Lord Henry's arm. "In that case, let our friendship be a caprice," he murmured, flushing at his own boldness, then stepped up on the platform and resumed his pose.

For the next quarter of an hour the studio remained in silence as Basil continued his work on the portrait. When he finally finished and

wrote down his name at the base of the portrait, Lord Henry came to examine it.

"It is one of the finest paintings of modern times," he said before calling out to Dorian.

The young man came and stood before the painting. A look of joy came into his eyes. Basil Hallward had always complimented his good looks. But he had never given much attention to this. But now he was seeing himself through Lord Henry's eyes. It was as though he had become aware of his good looks for the first time. But with this came another realisation. The good looks would fade away one day. This reality hit him like a stone.

Basil could not understand the meaning of Dorian Gray's silence and asked, "Did you not like the portrait?"

Lord Henry said, "Oh, he likes it. But whose property is it?"

"Dorian's, of course."

"How sad it is!" murmured Dorian Gray with his eyes still fixed upon his own portrait.

"How sad it is! I shall grow old, and horrible, and dreadful. But this picture will remain always young. It will never be older than this particular day of June ... If it were only the other way! If it were I who was to be always young, and the picture that was to grow old! For that — for that — I would give everything! Yes, there is nothing in the whole world I would not give! I would give my soul for that!" Basil did not like the idea and expressed his displeasure.

Dorian Gray turned and looked at him. "I believe you would, Basil. You like your art better than your friends. I am no more to you than a green bronze figure."

The painter stared in amazement. It was so unlike Dorian to speak like that. What had happened? He seemed quite angry. His face was flushed and his cheeks burning.

"Yes," Dorian continued, "I am less to you than your ivory Hermes or your silver Faun. You will like them always. How long will you like me? Till I have my first wrinkle, I suppose. I know, now, that when one loses one's good looks,

whatever they may be, one loses everything. Your picture has taught me that. Lord Henry Wotton is perfectly right. Youth is the only thing worth having. When I find that I am growing old, I shall kill myself." Basil was horrified at this reaction. He assured Dorian that he was a dear friend and certainly more important than superficial things like age and looks. But his words did not calm Dorian.

"I am jealous of everything whose beauty will not fade away. Why did you have to paint this Basil? Now it will mock me forever," said Dorian, his voice reflecting his sadness and anger.

Basil, by now, was quite disturbed at this turn of events. "You two have now made me hate my finest work, and I will destroy it. What is it but canvas and colour? I will not let it come across our three lives and mar them," he said bitterly to his two friends.

"Stop it Basil! Destroying something as beautiful as this would be nothing short of murder," Dorian said in exasperation.

This seemed to finally assure Basil that his

4

friend had indeed liked the painting. He told Dorian that he would send the painting to his place after it is varnished and framed.

Lord Henry was a silent spectator to the whole scene. "I adore simple pleasures," said Lord Henry. "They are the last refuge of the complex. But I don't like scenes, except on the stage. What absurd fellows you are, both of you! I wonder who it was defined man as a rational animal. It was the most premature definition ever given. Man is many things, but he is not rational. I am glad he is not, after all — though I wish you chaps would not squabble over the picture. You had much better let me have it, Basil. This silly boy doesn't really want it, and I really do."

As the three men sat down for tea, Lord Henry suggested that they go to the theatre. Basil immediately declined saying that he had a lot of work. The other reason was that he did not like to dress up in his fineries just to be seen in public. Dorian agreed to go with Sir Henry. Basil asked him to stay back for dinner instead,

but Dorian refused.

"It is rather late, and, as you have to dress, you had better lose no time. Goodbye, Harry. Goodbye, Dorian. Come and see me soon. Come tomorrow."

"Certainly."

"You won't forget?"

"No, of course not," cried Dorian.

"And ... Harry!"

"Yes, Basil?"

"Remember what I asked you when we were in the garden this morning?"

"I have forgotten it."

"I trust you."

"I wish I could trust myself," said Lord Henry, laughing. "Come, Mr Gray, my hansom is outside, and I can drop you at your own place. Goodbye, Basil. It has been a most interesting afternoon."

As the door closed behind them, the painter flung himself down on a sofa, and a look of pain came into his face.

Chapter Three

Enquiry

The next afternoon, Lord Henry decided to visit
his uncle, Lord Fermor. The ageing aristocrat was
a very wealthy man. He did not have to do much
work since his younger days. The properties and
businesses owned by his family brought him all
his earnings. Lord Fermor spent a lot of time at
the club and knew a lot of people. Lord Henry had
a reason for visiting him. He wanted to find out
more about his new acquaintance, Dorian Gray.
He said, "I know who he is. He is the last Lord
Kelso's grandson. His mother was a Devereux,
Lady Margaret Devereux. I want you to tell me

about his mother. What was she like? Whom did she marry? I have only just met him."

"Kelso's grandson!" echoed the old gentleman. "Kelso's grandson! ... Of course ... I knew his mother intimately. I believe I was at her christening. She was an extraordinarily beautiful girl, Margaret Devereux, and made all the men frantic by running away with a penniless young fellow — a mere nobody. Certainly. I remember the whole thing as if it happened yesterday. The poor chap was killed in a duel at Spa a few months after the marriage. There was an ugly story about it. They said Kelso got some rascally adventurer, some Belgian brute, to insult his son-in-law in public — paid him, sir, to do it, paid him. He brought his daughter back with him, I was told, and she never spoke to him again. Oh, yes; it was a bad business. The girl died, too, died within a year. So she left a son. If he is like his mother, he must be a good-looking chap."

"He is very good-looking," assented Lord Henry.

"I hope he will fall into proper hands," continued the old man. "He should have a pot of money waiting for him if Kelso did the right thing by him. His mother had money too. All the Selby property came to her, through her grandfather."

"Was Dorian's mother truly very beautiful?"

"Margaret Devereux was one of the loveliest creatures I ever saw, Harry."

Lord Henry had an invitation to his Aunt Agatha's house that day, so he excused himself and made his way there.

So that was the story of Dorian Gray's parentage. Crudely as it had been told to him, it had yet stirred him by its suggestion of a strange, almost modern romance. A beautiful woman risking everything for a mad passion. A few wild weeks of happiness cut short by a hideous, treacherous crime. Months of voiceless agony, and then a child born in pain. The mother snatched away by death, the boy left to solitude and the tyranny of an old and loveless man. Yes; it was an interesting background. It posed the lad, made him more perfect, as it were. Behind every exquisite thing that existed, there was something tragic. He would seek to dominate him – had already, indeed, half done so. He would make that wonderful spirit his own. There was something fascinating in this son of love and death.

"Late as usual, Harry," cried his aunt, shaking her head at him, when he finally reached her house.

In no time, Lord Henry had captured the attention of the other guests. They were quite stunned about his views on a wide range of topics. His opinions on the importance of giving in to impulses got the most attention.

"The only way to get back one's youth is to repeat mistakes," he said seriously.

"A delightful theory!" she exclaimed. "I must put it into practice."

"A dangerous theory!" came from Sir Thomas's tight lips.

All the while that Sir Henry spoke, he was aware of Dorian's attention on him. He knew that he had found an admirer in the young man. This seemed to give a new life to all that he had

to say. He completely won over his audience with his charm. Dorian was no exception.

The party ended when the Duchess announced that she had to leave. Her carriage had arrived and she had to pick up her husband. She invited Lord Henry for dinner and left the gathering. It was obvious that Lord Henry had made quite a few fans that day. Mr Erskine invited him to Treadley.

As he was passing out of the door, Dorian Gray touched him on the arm. "Let me come with you," he murmured.

"But I thought you had promised Basil Hallward to go and see him," answered Lord Henry.

"I would sooner come with you; yes, I feel I must come with you. Do let me. And you will promise to talk to me all the time? No one talks so wonderfully as you do."

"Ah! I have talked quite enough for today," said Lord Henry, smiling. "All I want now is to look at life. You may come and look at it with me, if you care to."

Chapter Four

Love

A month had gone by. Dorian Gray was in the library at Lord Henry's house, waiting for him. Just when Dorian was wondering whether he should leave, he heard the sound of the door. Happy that his friend had arrived, Dorian turned towards the door. He was surprised to find a woman standing there.

"I am afraid it is not Harry, Mr Gray," answered a shrill voice.

He glanced quickly round and rose to his feet. "I beg your pardon. I thought—"

"You thought it was my husband. It is only his wife. You must let me introduce myself. I know

you quite well by your photographs. And I saw you with him the other night at the opera."

"Yes; it was at dear Lohengrin. I like Wagner's music better than anybody's. It is so loud that one can talk the whole time without other people hearing what one says. That is a great advantage, don't you think so, Mr Gray?"

Dorian smiled and shook his head, "I am afraid I don't think so, Lady Henry. I never talk during music — at least, during good music. If one hears bad music, it is one's duty to drown it in conversation."

"Isn't that Harry's opinion? I always hear his friends expressing his opinions," pointed out Lady Henry. "But here is Harry! Harry, I came in to look for you, to ask you something — I forget what it was — and I found Mr Gray here. We have had such a pleasant chat about music. We have quite the same ideas. No; I think our ideas are quite different. But he has been most pleasant. I am so glad I've seen him."

"I am charmed, my love, quite charmed," said Lord Henry, elevating his dark, crescent-shaped

eyebrows and looking at them both with an amused smile. "So sorry I am late, Dorian."

"I am afraid I must be going," exclaimed Lady Henry, breaking an awkward silence with her silly sudden laugh. "I have promised to drive with the duchess. Goodbye, Mr Gray. Goodbye, Harry. You are dining out, I suppose? So am I. Perhaps I shall see you at Lady Thornbury's." As soon as she left the room, Lord Henry said, "Do not get married, Dorian. Men get married because they are bored and women because they are curious. Both are disappointed."

"I don't think I am likely to marry, Harry. I am too much in love. That is one of your aphorisms. I am putting it into practice, as I do everything that you say."

"Who are you in love with?" asked Lord Henry after a pause.

"With an actress," said Dorian Gray, blushing.

Lord Henry shrugged his shoulders. "That is a rather commonplace debut."

"You would not say so if you saw her, Harry."

"Who is she?"

"Her name is Sibyl Vane."

"Never heard of her."

"No one has. People will some day, however. She is a genius."

"My dear boy, no woman is a genius. Women are a decorative sex. They never have anything to say, but they say it charmingly. Women represent the triumph of matter over mind, just as men represent the triumph of mind over morals."

"Harry, how can you?"

"My dear Dorian, it is quite true. I am analysing women at present, so I ought to know. The subject is not so abstruse as I thought it was. I find that, ultimately, there are only two kinds of women, the plain and the coloured. The plain women are very useful. If you want to gain a reputation for respectability, you have merely to take them down to supper. The other women are very charming. They commit one mistake, however. They paint in order to try and look young. Our grandmothers painted in order to try and talk brilliantly. Rouge and esprit used to go together. That is all over now. As long as a woman can look ten years younger than her own daughter, she is perfectly satisfied. As for conversation, there are only five women in London worth talking to, and two of these can't be admitted into decent society. However, tell me about your genius. How long have you known her?"

"Ah! Harry, your views terrify me."

"Never mind that. How long have you known her?"

"About three weeks."

"And where did you come across her?"

"It never would have happened if I had not met you. You filled me with a wild desire to know everything about life. Well, one evening, I went out and wandered eastward of London, soon losing my way in a labyrinth of grimy streets and black grassless squares. About half-past eight, I passed by an absurd little theatre. A hideous Jew, standing outside the gate asked me, 'Have a box, my Lord?' He was such a monster. You will laugh at me, I know, but I really went in and paid a whole guinea for the stage-box. To the present day I can't make out why I did so; and yet if I hadn't—my dear Harry, if I hadn't—I should have missed the greatest romance of my life. I see you are laughing. It is horrid of you!"

"I am amused, but please carry on," said Lord Henry, barely able to conceal his laughter.

"This play was good enough for us, Harry. It was Romeo and Juliet. I must admit that I was rather annoyed at the idea of seeing Shakespeare done in such a wretched hole of a place. The actors of the play were horrid, except Juliet! She was the loveliest thing I had ever seen in my life. You know how a voice can stir one. Your voice and the voice of Sibyl Vane are two things that I shall never forget. When I close my eyes, I hear them, and each of them says something different. I don't know which to follow. Why should I not love her? Harry, I do love her. She is everything to me in life. Night after night I go to see her play. One evening she is Rosalind, and the next evening she is Imogen. How different an actress is from a common woman! Harry! Why didn't you tell me that the only thing worth loving is an actress?"

"Because I have loved so many of them, Dorian."

"Oh, yes, horrid people with dyed hair and painted faces. I wish now I had not told you about Sibyl Vane."

"You could not have helped telling me, Dorian. All through your life you will tell me everything you do. What are your actual relations with Sibyl Vane?"

"She is pure, Harry!"

"I suppose she will belong to you some day. When one is in love, one always begins by deceiving one's self, and one always ends by deceiving others. That is what the world calls a romance. You know her, at any rate, I suppose?"

"Of course I know her. On the first night I was at the theatre, the horrid old Jew came round to the box after the performance was over and offered to take me behind the scenes and introduce me to her. The third night, she had been playing Rosalind. I could not help going round. I had thrown her some flowers, and she had looked at me—at least I fancied that she had. The old Jew was persistent. He seemed determined to take me behind, so I consented.

Sybil was so shy and so gentle. Her eyes opened wide in exquisite wonder when I told her what I thought of her performance, and she seemed quite unconscious of her power. She said quite simply to me, 'You look more like a prince. I must call you Prince Charming.'"

"Miss Sibyl certainly knows how to pay compliments," said Lord Henry sarcastically interrupting Dorian's narrative.

But Dorian's admiration for the young woman was unwavering. "Tonight she will be Imogen. Tomorrow she will be Juliet," muttered Dorian.

"And when is she Sibyl Vane?" asked his friend with a strange note in his voice.

"Never," replied Dorian. "How horrid you are! She is all the great heroines of the world in one. She is more than an individual. You laugh, but I tell you she has genius. I love her, and I must make her love me. You, who know all the secrets of life, tell me how to charm Sibyl Vane to love me!" He was walking up and down the room as he spoke. Hectic spots of red burned on his cheeks. He was terribly excited.

"And what do you propose to do?" said Lord Henry at last.

"I want you and Basil to come with me some night and see her act. I have not the slightest fear of the result. You are certain to acknowledge her genius. Then, we must get her out of the Jew's hands. She is bound to him for three years — at least for two years and eight months — from the present time. I shall have to pay him something, of course. When all that is settled, I shall take a West End theatre and bring her out properly. She will make the world as mad as she has made me."

"Well, what night shall we go?"

"Let me see. Today is Tuesday. Let us fix tomorrow. She plays Juliet tomorrow."

"All right. The Bristol at 8 o'clock; and I will get Basil."

"Not eight, Harry, please. Half-past six. We must be there before the curtain rises. You must see her in the first act, where she meets Romeo."

"Shall you see Basil between this and then? Or shall I write to him?"

"Dear Basil! I have not laid eyes on him for

a week. It is rather horrid of me, as he has sent me my portrait in the most wonderful frame, specially designed by himself, and, though I am a little jealous of the picture for being a whole month younger than I am, I must admit that I delight in it. Perhaps you had better write to him. I don't want to see him alone. He says things that annoy me. He gives me good advice."

Lord Henry smiled. Soon after this, Dorian left to meet Sibyl.

Lord Henry sat quietly for a long time thinking about Dorian Gray. The young man's passionate response to things spoke of the strong influence he had begun to have on him; Dorian now seemed to be his own creation; a puppet to his way of thinking. He admitted to himself that it was a delight to watch him.

He left for his dinner soon after.

A telegram was waiting for him when he returned from his outing. It was from Dorian Gray. He informed his friend that he had got engaged to Sibyl Vane.

Chapter Five

Sibyl Vane

"Mother, Mother, I am so happy!" whispered Sibyl, burying her face in the lap of the faded, tired-looking woman.

Mrs Vane winced and said, "Happy! I am only happy, Sibyl, when I see you act. You must not think of anything but your acting. Mr Isaacs has been very good to us, and we owe him money."

Sibyl cried, "What does money matter? Love is more than money."

"Mr Isaacs has advanced us fifty pounds to pay off our debts and to get a proper outfit for James. You must not forget that, Sibyl. Fifty pounds is a very large sum. Mr Isaacs has been most considerate."

"He is not a gentleman, Mother, and I hate the way he talks to me," said the girl rising to her feet and going over to the window.

"I don't know how we could manage without him," answered the elder woman querulously.

Sibyl Vane tossed her head and laughed. "We don't want him anymore, Mother. Prince Charming rules life for us now. I love him," she said simply.

"Foolish child! Foolish child!" cried her mother.

"You are too young to fall in love. Besides, you do not know anything about this man ... not even his name. This is really foolish. Your brother James is going away to Australia. I have so much to think about now," finished her mother in a huff. The ageing actress's face had an exaggerated expression of worry.

Just then, the front door opened and a tall, stout man came into the room. With a squeal of happiness, Sybil ran and hugged him.

"I want you to come out for a walk with me," said the tall man, looking at his sister tenderly, before adding, "I am not going to see this horrible city of London again."

"Don't say that. I am sure you will return to London as a rich man," corrected his mother.

"I want to make enough money to make sure that Sybil and you don't have to work on the stage," said James gruffly.

Sybil didn't like to see her brother upset. She suggested that they walk to the park. She then went to her room to get ready. She was humming all the way.

"Mother, you must watch over Sybil. I have heard that a gentleman comes to the theatre every day. He even goes backstage to speak to her. That is not right," he said sternly.

"You don't understand James. We have to get used to a lot of attention when we work on the stage. I used to get many bouquets when I was younger. The man is a gentleman. Besides, he looks rich. I am not sure whether Sybil likes him," said his mother, once again displaying her shallow nature.

"Watch over Sybil, Mother," James repeated, his voice reflecting his worry.

But Mrs Vane saw no reason to worry. She did not think there was anything wrong in her daughter getting friendly with the gentleman. Especially, because he looked like a wealthy man.

Before James could respond to this Sybil returned and the two left for a walk. As they walked, Sybil in a happy voice spoke of all the ways her brother could become a rich man in Australia. James was not paying attention to anything she said. All he could think about was what would happen to Sybil when he was away.

"Do not forget us, James," said Sybil finally drawing her brother's attention.

"You are the one who is likely to forget me," said James. His voice was a mixture of sternness and tenderness. He added, "I have heard that you have a new friend. Why have you not told me about him? I do not think he is good for you."

"Don't say that, James. I love him," cried Sybil.

"Why, you don't even know his name," answered the lad. "Who is he? I have a right to know."

"He is called Prince Charming. Oh! you silly boy! You should never forget it. If you only saw him, you would think him the most wonderful person in the world. Some day you will meet him — when you come back from Australia. You will like him so much. Everybody likes him, and I ... love him. I wish you could come to the theatre tonight. He is going to be there, and I am to play Juliet. To have him sitting there! Even Mr Isaacs will announce me as a revelation." "Please be careful about him," said James, his voice clearly reflected his anxiousness. He knew he would not be around to take care of her.

"You dear old Jim, you talk as if you were a hundred. Someday you will be in love yourself. Then you will know what it is. Don't look so sulky. Surely you should be glad to think that, though you are going away, you leave me happier

than I have ever been before. Life has been hard for us both, terribly hard and difficult. But it will be different now. You are going to a new world, and I have found one." As they continued to talk about Jim's future, Sibyl noticed Dorian drive by in an open carriage with two ladies.

"There he is," she pointed out to her brother excitedly.

But the carriage went out of sight before James could see him.

"If he harms you in anyway, I am going to kill him," said James angrily. The anger in his voice caused Sybil to shudder in fear.

But she put aside her fears. She knew that her brother was a good man. He would never harm anyone; least of all the man she loved.

When they returned home, Mrs Vane was waiting for them. Sybil went to her room upstairs and James stayed back for his meal. He was very worried about his sister. "Mother, I have something to ask you," he said. Her eyes wandered vaguely about the room. She made no

answer. "Tell me the truth. I have a right to know. Were you married to my father?"

"No," she answered.

"My father was a scoundrel then!" cried the lad, clenching his fists.

She shook her head and said, "I knew he was not free. We loved each other very much. If he had lived, he would have made provision for us. Don't speak against him, my son. He was your father, and a gentleman. Indeed, he was highly connected."

"So is the man Sibyl loves. Look out for her, Mother. If he harms her in any way, I will kill him when I come back," he said angrily.

Mrs Vane dismissed his fear as unnecessary and James left soon after.

Chapter Six

The Engagement

Lord Henry and Basil were in the private dining room at the Bristol. They had come for dinner. Dorian was going to join them in some time.

"Have you heard the news Basil?" asked Lord Henry.

"What news? I have no interest in politics. The people in that field won't even make good subjects for my paintings," joked Basil.

"Dorian Gray is engaged to be married," informed Lord Henry.

Basil was stunned to hear this news.

"To whom?"

"To some little actress or other."

"I can't believe it. Dorian is far too sensible. It would be absurd for him to marry so much beneath him."

"If you want to make him marry this girl, tell him that, Basil. He is sure to do it then. Whenever a man does a thoroughly stupid thing, it is always from the noblest motives."

"I hope the girl is good, Harry. I don't want to see Dorian tied to some vile creature, who might degrade his nature and ruin his intellect."

"Oh, she is better than good—she is beautiful," murmured Lord Henry, sipping a glass of vermouth and orange-bitters. "Dorian says she is beautiful, and he is not often wrong about things of that kind. Your portrait of him has quickened his appreciation of the personal appearance of other people. It has had that excellent effect, amongst others. We are to see her tonight, if that boy doesn't forget his appointment."

"But do you approve of it, Harry?" asked the painter.

"I never approve, or disapprove, of anything now. It is an absurd attitude to take towards life. With my experience of marriage, I hope that Dorian Gray will make this girl his wife, passionately adore her for six months, and then suddenly become fascinated by someone else. He would be a wonderful study."

"You don't mean a single word of all that, Harry. If Dorian Gray's life were spoiled, no one would be sorrier than yourself."

Just then Dorian arrived. He looked very happy.

"You both must congratulate me," he said, his face glowing.

"I will not forgive you for not telling me about your engagement earlier," Basil complained.

"But first you must tell us how this whole thing happened," Lord Henry cut in.

"There is really not much to tell," cried Dorian as they took their seats at the small round table. "What happened was simply this. After I left you yesterday evening, I went to the theatre. Sibyl was playing Rosalind. You should have seen her! When she came on in her boy's clothes, she was perfectly wonderful. She is simply a born artist. I sat in the dingy box absolutely enthralled. After the performance was over, I went behind and spoke to her. As we were sitting together, suddenly there came into her eyes a look that I had never seen there before. My lips moved towards hers. We kissed each other. I can't describe to you what I felt at that moment. It seemed to me that all my life had been narrowed to one perfect point of rose-coloured joy. I have been right, Basil, haven't I, to take my love out of poetry and to find my wife in Shakespeare's plays? Lips that Shakespeare taught to speak have whispered their secret in my ear. I have had the arms of Rosalind around me, and kissed Juliet on the mouth. I did not make a formal proposal. I told her that I loved her. She responded by saying that she was not worthy to become my wife. Can you imagine anybody being more

worthy than her?"Dorian responded innocently, his voice reflecting his affection for Sybil.

"It is a funny thing. But it is always the women who propose to us," pointed out Lord Henry.

"Harry you are dreadful. I don't know why I still like you," said Dorian interrupting his friend's disparaging comments on women.

It was then decided that they would leave for the theatre immediately. Dorian drove with Lord Henry and Basil travelled in his own carriage.

Chapter Seven

The Play

The theatre was very crowded and the fat Jew manager who met them at the door was beaming from ear to ear with an oily tremulous smile. He escorted them to their box with a sort of pompous humility, waving his fat jewelled hands and talking at the top of his voice. Dorian hated him all the more. He was now more determined to take Sybil away from this horrible place. The manager escorted them to a box. The place was really hot. The crowd in the gallery below comprised all the coarse population of London. They laughed loudly and were generally very noisy.

"An interesting place to find the love of one's life," mocked Lord Henry.

Dorian was quick to respond, "Yes, this is where I found her. When you see her you will forget all these rough people around here. When the curtain rises, you will see the girl to whom I am going to dedicate the rest of my life."

A quarter of an hour later, the curtain rose and Sybil Vane stepped on to the stage. The auditorium broke into applause. Yes, she was certainly lovely to look at — one of the loveliest creatures, Lord Henry thought, that he had ever seen. There was something of the fawn in her shy grace and startled eyes.

The play began. The actor who played Romeo entered the scene with his friends. Sybil's beauty made her stand apart from everybody. The other actors looked shabby in front of her. Yet, she was curiously listless. The brief dialogue that followed the scene at the first meeting of Romeo and Juliet, were spoken in a thoroughly artificial manner. The voice was exquisite, but from the point of

view of tone it was absolutely false. It was wrong in colour. It took away all the life from the verse. It made the passion unreal. Dorian Gray grew pale as he watched her. He was puzzled and anxious. Neither of his friends dared to say anything to him. She seemed to them to be absolutely incompetent. They were horribly disappointed. They waited for the second act, but she failed to deliver yet again.

Even the common uneducated audience of the pit and gallery lost their interest in the play. They got restless and began to talk loudly and to whistle. The Jew manager, who was standing at the back of the dress-circle, stamped and swore with rage. The only person unmoved was the girl herself. "She is very beautiful, Dorian. But she cannot act," said Lord Henry as he got up to leave at the end of a scene.

"I am sorry I made you waste your evening," Dorian said in anger.

"I think she is ill, Dorian. We will come another night," said Basil, trying to calm Dorian.

But Dorian was really upset.

"Last night she was an artiste, but today she is a common actress," said Dorian bitterly, expressing his disappointment.

"They are both simply forms of imitation," remarked Lord Henry. "But do let us go. Dorian, you must not stay here any longer. It is not good for one's morals to see bad acting. She is very lovely, and if she knows as little about life as she does about acting, she will be a delightful experience. Come to the club with Basil and myself. We will smoke cigarettes and drink to the beauty of Sibyl Vane. She is beautiful. What more can you want?"

But Dorian was in no mood to do so. He told his friends that he just wanted to be alone. They understood and left.

The play continued and so did Dorian's misery. Sybil's acting made him miserable but he still continued to watch. When the play finally came to an end, there were very few people left

in the auditorium. Dorian decided to go and meet Sybil backstage.

A terrible performance like the one he had witnessed should have made Sybil gloomy. Instead, the young woman was smiling. There was a joy on her face that stunned Dorian.

"Didn't I acted terribly tonight Dorian?" asked Sybil. There was no mistaking the smile in her voice.

"You were terrible. Do you know how I suffered as I watched you on stage?" responded Dorian.

"You didn't understand why?" asked Sybil.

"Understand what?" he asked, angrily.

"Why I was so bad tonight. Why I shall always be bad. Why I shall never act well again."

When Dorian's face grew sour, she cried, "Dorian, before I knew you, acting was the one reality of my life. It was only in the theatre that I lived. I thought that it was all true. I believed in everything. The common people who acted with me seemed to me to be godlike. The painted scenes were my world. Then you came and you freed my soul from prison. You taught me what reality really is. You had made me understand what love really is. And it is nothing like the lines of Shakespeare."

"You have killed my love for you," Dorian said bitterly before continuing, "I loved you because you were brilliant on stage. But now you are shallow and stupid. You do not know anything about love, if you say that it has ruined your art. I do not want to see you again. You are nothing today but a terrible actress who just has a pretty face."

Sybil was horrified at this anger and the cruelty in his words. She thought that Dorian was just joking. She put her hand on his arm but he pushed her away.

Sybil realised that he was leaving. She tried to stop him by saying that she would improve her acting. But Dorian did not want to listen to her. The young girl's tears and imploring now annoyed him. He just wanted to leave the place and never set eyes on her again.

"You have disappointed me. I don't want to see you ever again," said Dorian harshly and left the place, leaving a distraught Sybil sobbing on the floor.

Dorian wandered the streets of London for hours. He went towards the Covent Garden and watched as traders prepared to set up their shops. The city was bathed in sunlight by the time he reached his house.

He threw himself into a chair and began to think. Suddenly there flashed across his mind what he had said in Basil Hallward's studio the day the picture had been finished. Yes, he remembered it perfectly. He had uttered a mad wish that he himself might remain young, and the portrait grow old; that his own beauty might be untarnished and the face on the canvas bear the burden of his passions and his sins; that the painted image might be seared with the lines of suffering and thought, and that he might keep all the delicate bloom and loveliness of his then just-conscious boyhood. Surely his wish had

not been fulfilled? Such things were impossible It seemed monstrous even to think of them. And, yet, there was the picture before him, with the touch of cruelty in the mouth.

Cruelty! Had he been cruel? It was the girl's fault, not his. He had dreamed of her as a great artist, had given his love to her because he had thought her great. Then she had disappointed him. She had been shallow and unworthy. And, yet, a feeling of infinite regret came over him, as he thought of her lying at his feet sobbing like a little child. Why should he trouble about Sibyl Vane? She was nothing to him now.

He looked at the picture now and he remembered how it had made him aware of his good looks, how it had taught him to admire perfection. Would it now teach him to hate the person that he was? With this thought came great regret.

He thought of Sybil. He remembered how she fell sobbing to the floor as he walked away.

He looked at the change in the picture. He realised that if the picture indeed reflected his soul then it would change even further. He felt pity that the picture would lose its perfection; every sin he committed would leave a visible mark on the portrait. For some reason this seemed to disturb Dorian greatly.

Then he decided that he would not meet Lord Henry anymore. He told himself that he is the one who had changed his life in Basil's garden that day. Dorian decided that he would go and meet Sybil later in the day. He would apologise to her for his previous cold behaviour.

With this thought, he covered the painting with a screen, as if to hide the change that had come over in the portrait and went to bed for some rest.

Chapter Eight

Death

Dorian slept till late in the afternoon. He woke up feeling drowsy. Victor came in softly with a cup of tea, and a pile of letters, on a small tray of old Sevres china, and drew back the olive-satin curtains, with their shimmering blue lining, that hung in front of the three tall windows. Dorian sat up, and having sipped some tea, turned over his letters.

He noticed that there was one from Lord Henry. He decided to ignore it, in the face of the resolution he had made earlier in the day. He wrote down a passionate letter of regret to Sybil. As soon as he was dressed, he went into the

library and sat down to a light French breakfast that had been laid out for him on a small round table close to the open window. Suddenly his eye fell on the screen that he had placed in front of the portrait, and he started. He got up and locked both doors. At least he would be alone when he looked upon the mask of his shame. Then he drew the screen aside and saw himself face-to-face. It was perfectly true. The portrait had altered.

Just then there was a knock on the door and he realised that it was Lord Henry. Dorian did not want to meet anybody, especially this friend. But Lord Henry continued to knock till Dorian opened the door.

"I am very sorry for everything, Dorian," said his usually merry friend.

"You mean about Sybil?" asked Dorian.

"Yes, of course. Did you go and meet her after the play? Did you both have a confrontation?" asked Lord Henry, with a strange urgency in his voice.

"I was horrible to her, Harry. But it also taught me a lot about myself. I know now that

it is important to be true to one's conscience. I will make amends for what I have done," said Dorian confidently.

"And how will you do that?" asked Lord Henry, his voice reflecting surprise.

"I will marry Sybil Vane," announced Dorian.

"What! Haven't you read the letter I sent to you this morning," said Lord Henry before walking to his friend and taking his friend's hand and announcing gravely, "Sybil Vane is dead."

"That is a horrible lie," Dorian lashed out.

"It is true. I wrote to you telling you not to see anyone before I arrived. There is bound to be an enquiry into this. I suppose nobody in the theatre knows your name. There is bound to be a scandal about this," explained Lord Henry.

Dorian could not believe his ears. Lord Henry explained how it had all happened. He said, "I have no doubt it was not an accident, Dorian, though it must be put in that way to the public. It seems that as she was leaving the theatre with her mother, about half-past twelve or so, she said she had forgotten something upstairs. They waited some time for her, but she did not come down again. They ultimately found her lying dead on the floor of her dressing room. She had swallowed something by mistake, some dreadful thing they use at theatres. I don't know what it was, but it had either prussic acid or white lead in it. I should fancy it was prussic acid, as she seems to have died instantaneously." "So I murdered Sybil Vane," said a horrified Dorian.

Lord Henry assured him that he was not to be blamed for her death and told him that he would have been miserable if he had married her. Dorian admitted that he did not feel as affected by this tragedy as he should have. Lord Henry invited him for dinner and then to an opera afterwards. Dorian agreed to go.

After his friend left, Dorian sat looking at the painting. A number of thoughts ran through his head. The tragedy of last night, Sybil's suicide, had been reflected in the painting long before he had known about it. The sneer on the face had probably appeared right at the moment when Sybil had drunk poison.

Since Basil had given him the painting, he had spent hours looking at it—marveling at its beauty. Dorian now asked himself: Would the painting now change with every impulse he gave in to? Would it one day become so ugly that he would have to hide it away from every eye? He asked himself how he would feel if the changes occurred right before his eyes. This thought made him shudder.

These thoughts also brought in another realisation; something that made him very happy —his good looks would remain with him forever. Like Greek gods, he would be strong and healthy forever. How did it matter what happened to this painting, he asked himself. He would be perfect. Forever.

With this happy thought, he decided to go get dressed to meet Lord Henry at the Opera house. His valet was waiting for him in his room. An hour later he was at the opera; all thoughts about the painting and his soul had disappeared from his mind. At least for the time being!

Chapter Nine

A Change

Dorian was having his breakfast the next morning when Basil arrived. "I am so glad I have found you, Dorian," he said gravely. "I called last night, and they told me you were at the opera. Did you go down and see the girl's mother? Poor woman! What a state she must be in! And her only child, too! What did she say about it all?"

"My dear Basil, how do I know? I was at the opera, meeting new people," murmured Dorian. "How can you enjoy the opera when the girl you loved has not yet found a peaceful grave?" asked Basil incredulously, unable to hide the horror in his voice.

"Oh, Basil, what is past is past," responded Dorian.

Basil was stunned that Dorian could refer to the day before as "past". He was amazed at the way Dorian had changed. Dorian had a perfectly sound argument for his attitude. He explained that it is only the petty people who cling on to an emotion. A man who has mastery over himself should be able to move on.

Basil listened dumbfounded as his friend spoke about Sybil in the most flippant way. According to Dorian, she had always acted in tragedies on the stage. In her death, like Juliet, she had been finally united with her art. The cruelty and the callousness of emotions that Dorian displayed once again amazed the painter. He realised that the young man had changed dramatically and was now a completely different person.

"The investigation into her death will be held this afternoon. Have you been summoned?" Basil asked finally.

"They don't know my name," Dorian said casually.

"Surely she knew your name," asked Basil in surprise.

"She only knew that my name was Dorian. Anyway, she called me her Prince Charming. She even told me that this is the name she used for me when her acquaintances enquired. Isn't that rather sweet? You must paint a portrait of her for me, so that I don't forget her," Dorian said nonchalantly.

At this moment Basil noticed that Dorian's portrait was covered with a screen.

A cry of terror broke from Dorian Gray's lips, and he rushed between the painter and the screen. "Basil," he said, looking very pale, "you must not look at it. I don't wish you to."

"Not look at my own work! You are not serious. Why shouldn't I look at it?" exclaimed Hallward, laughing.

"If you try to look at it, Basil, on my word of honour I will never speak to you again as long as

I live. I don't offer any explanation, and you are not to ask for any."

Hallward was thunderstruck. He looked at Dorian Gray in absolute amazement. He had never seen him like this before.

"Dorian!"

"Don't speak!"

"It seems rather absurd that I shouldn't see my own work, especially as I am going to exhibit it in Paris in the autumn. I shall probably have to give it another coat of varnish before that, so I must see it some day, and why not today?"

"You want to exhibit it?" exclaimed Dorian.

"Have you noticed something in the painting that you had not noticed earlier?" Basil asked, causing Dorian's face to reflect his panic. "I can see that you have," the painter continued noticing the trembling hands of his friend. "I was absolutely obsessed with this picture and you as I was painting it. I am sure you realise that as you look at the painting now. It clearly shows how you had become my idol. The perfect representation of my art," Basil revealed.

Dorian breathed a sigh of relief. He knew that Basil had no idea about the secret of the painting. He had no intention of letting Basil see the painting and noticing the changes that had come over it. He pretended to have taken offence to the painter's revelation. He told Basil that he would never become a subject of his paintings again. Basil was so embarrassed that he left almost immediately. Dorian Gray's portrait behind the screen was forgotten. The young man decided that it was time he hid the painting from everybody's eyes.

Chapter Ten

The Schoolroom

Dorian called his servant, Victor. He asked him to call two men from the shop that framed paintings. After Victor left for his errand, Dorian called his housekeeper Mrs Leaf. He asked her for the keys of the schoolroom that was located at the top of the house.

He winced at the mention of his grandfather. He had hateful memories of him. "That does not matter," he answered. "I simply want to see the place — that is all. Give me the key."

"And here is the key, sir," said the old lady, going over the contents of her bunch with tremulously uncertain hands. "Here is the key.

I'll have it off the bunch in a moment. But you don't think of living up there, sir, and you so comfortable here?"

"No, no," he cried petulantly. "Thank you, Leaf. That will do."

After Mrs Leaf left Dorian, his eye fell on a large, purple satin coverlet heavily embroidered with gold, a splendid piece of late seventeenth-century Venetian work that belonged to his grandfather. He decided to wrap the painting with it and put away the painting.

As he looked at the painting again, he wondered whether it had changed again. Just then Victor came in to say that the men from the shop were here. Dorian did not want his butler to know where he would be putting the painting. So he scribbled a note to Lord Henry and asked Victor to take it to him and wait there till his friend sent back a reply.

Mr Hubbard, the owner of the store, had also come with his men. Like most of Dorian's acquaintances, he too was very fond of the young man. Dorian informed him that he did not want anything framed. He just wanted to move a picture to the top of the house.

Dorian asked the men to be very careful as they carried the picture up the stairs.

"Something of a load to carry, sir," gasped the little man when they reached the top landing. And he wiped his shiny forehead.

"I am afraid it is rather heavy," murmured Dorian as he unlocked the door that opened into the room that was to keep for him the curious secret of his life and hide his soul from the eyes of men.

As Dorian looked around the room, he remembered his lonely childhood here. He told himself that this was the perfect place to hide the picture. Nobody would be able to see it here. The picture would grow ugly and old here and nobody would see the changes. Dorian told himself that over the years this image of him would age; the hair would lose its shine, the cheeks would become hollow, there would be crow's feet near the eyes, wrinkles around the neck.

No, he decided, the portrait definitely could not be seen by another.

When Mr Hubbard asked to see the picture, Dorian refused saying that it would not interest him.

When the men had left, Dorian locked the door of the room and placed the key in his pocket. He felt safe now. No one would ever look upon the horrible thing. No eye would ever see his shame.

After the men left Dorian came back to his library. The day's newspaper was on the table. It also had a note from Lord Henry and a book bound in yellow paper. So he knew that victor was back in the house. He wondered if he had met the men on their way out. He was bound to eventually notice that the picture was not there in the room anymore. Dorian wondered if Victor would try to go to the school room. He had heard several stories of rich men being blackmailed by their servants who had found out their secrets.

He dismissed the thought to pick up the newspaper. There was news regarding the investigation on the death of Sybil Vane.

Dorian put all his distressing thoughts aside and picked up the book that Lord Henry had sent. Reading just a few pages, Dorian was fascinated. It was the story of a young Parisian who lived in the nineteenth century. The man wanted to experience all of life's pleasures. He did not care to decide between what was right and what was wrong. Dorian also noticed that a fragrance of incense clung to the pages. And this only added to the charm of the book and Dorian could not put it down.

He realised how long he had been reading only when Victor reminded him that he had to go to the club.

"I am sorry. The book you sent made me lose all sense of time," said Dorian to his friend Lord Henry who was waiting for him at the club.

"I knew you would like it," said his friend with a smile.

"I didn't say I liked it. I said it fascinated me. There is great difference between the two," Dorian corrected him as they walked into the dining room.

Chapter Eleven

The Mystery

For years, Dorian Gray could not free himself from the influence of this book. Or perhaps it would be more accurate to say that he never sought to free himself from it. He procured from Paris no less than nine large-paper copies of the first edition, and had them bound in different colours, so that they might suit his various moods. The hero, the wonderful young Parisian in whom the romantic and the scientific temperaments were so strangely blended, became to him a kind of prefiguring type of himself. And, indeed, the whole book seemed to him to contain the story of his own life, written before he had lived it. For the wonderful beauty

that had so fascinated Basil Hallward, and many others besides him, seemed never to leave him. Even those who had heard the most evil things against him — and from time to time strange rumours about his mode of life crept through London and became the chatter of the clubs — could not believe anything to his dishonour when they saw him. He had always the look of one who had kept himself unspotted from the world. Men who talked grossly became silent when Dorian Gray entered the room. There was something in the purity of his face that rebuked them. His mere presence seemed to recall to them the memory of the innocence that they had tarnished. They wondered how one so charming and graceful as he was could have escaped the stain of an age that was at once sordid and sensual. At times after returning home late in the night, Dorian would go up to the schoolroom to see the picture. The picture had grown ugly, reflecting his various sins and his age, with the passing years. Dorian would hold a mirror in front of him and compare

his good looks with that of the ugly portrait. As time passed, he became more obsessed with his good looks and more fascinated with how ugly his soul was becoming. He would, at times, keenly follow the details of the deterioration of the portrait; he would ask himself what kind of change was more horrible and dramatic — the change brought about by age or the change that was brought about by sin.

At times he would disappear for days. Nobody knew what he did then. He could be indulging one of his several romantic liaisons. Or he could be present in one of the disrepute taverns near the docks — places he frequented under an assumed name.

Sometimes during the sleepless nights he would think of how he had corrupted his soul. But these were rare moments. He was too caught up in the hedonistic discovery of life.

Back in London, he would often have huge parties and invite the Londoners. The people were fascinated by the meticulous arrangements

of these dinners. Those who came into contact with him were captivated by the mysterious air around him. The young men especially wanted to be like him.

Dorian was an intelligent man. In these years he also got busy studying about everything that fascinated him. He studied about perfumes and how they affected people. He also spent a lot of time and money learning about music, jewellery and tapestries—all this as he spent more time reading the young Parisian's story.

Chapter Twelve

Train to Paris

It was on the ninth of November, the eve of his own thirty-eighth birthday, as he often remembered afterwards.

He was walking home about 11 o'clock from Lord Henry's, where he had been dining, and was wrapped in heavy furs as the night was cold and foggy. He spotted Basil Hallward. A strange sense of fear, for which he could not account, came over him. He made no sign of recognition and went on quickly in the direction of his own house. But Basil had seen him and called out, "Dorian! What an extraordinary piece of luck! I have been waiting for you in your library ever

since 9 o'clock. Finally, I took pity on your tired servant and told him to go to bed, as he let me out. I am off to Paris by the midnight train, and I particularly wanted to see you before I left. I thought it was you, or rather your fur coat, as you passed me. But I wasn't quite sure. Didn't you recognise me?"

"In this fog, my dear Basil? Why, I can't even recognise Grosvenor Square. I believe my house is somewhere about here, but I don't feel at all certain about it. I am sorry you are going away, as I have not seen you for ages. But I suppose you will be back soon?"

"No, I am going to be out of England for 6 months. I intend to take a studio in Paris and shut myself up till I have finished a great picture I have in my head. However, it wasn't about myself I wanted to talk. Here we are at your door. Let me come in for a moment. I have something to say to you."

"But won't you miss your train?" Dorian tried to sound polite as he opened the front door with his key. Basil did not notice his displeasure.

"I have a lot of time. It is only 11 yet and the train does not leave till 12:15. I was heading to the club to look for you," Basil supplied as he followed Dorian into the house.

"Do you know what dreadful things are being said about you in London?" asked Basil at once.

"I don't have any interest in listening to scandals about myself. It is only scandals about others that interest me," Dorian said flippantly.

Basil ignored Dorian's callousness and told him the horrible stories he had heard about him.

"Every gentleman is interested in his good name. I am sure you do not want people to talk about you as a vile person. Of course, you have a position in society—and a lot of wealth. But that is not everything. But I cannot believe these rumours when I see you. Sin is something that leaves its mark on a man's face. It cannot be hidden. But you, Dorian, with your pure, bright and innocent face. I cannot believe anything against you," Basil said with an excited tremor in his voice.

He asked Dorian why so many of his friends were not willing to see him now. There was a rumour that he had been responsible for the suicide of a young man. And another man, who was considered to be his friend, had run away from England with his reputation completely ruined. He questioned Dorian how Lord Henry's sister, Lady Gwendolen, had acquired a bad name because of her association with him. No lady in London was now willing to be seen with her.

"Watch out Basil. You are going too far." There was now an anger in Dorian's voice.

"I must speak and you must listen," said Basil agitatedly before adding, "I want you to have a clean name. I want you to get rid of the dreadful people you associate with. Don't be indifferent to all these things.

There were other admonishments following which Basil urged Dorian to mend his ways.

"I don't want to believe the stories about you. I know you cannot do these things. But," he

paused before adding, "do I really know you? I wish I could see your soul."

"You want to see my soul?" Dorian asked, his face growing pale.

"Yes, I wish I could. But only God can do that," Basil said, his voice reflecting his sadness.

"But you will see it tonight?" said Dorian breaking into a strange laugh. There was a pride in his voice that Basil could not understand.

Dorian then told him that he would now show him what he thought only God could see. Basil asked him to stop saying such strange things. He just wanted Dorian to tell him that all the rumours that he had heard were untrue.

"You will get all your answers upstairs. I keep a diary and it never leaves the upstairs room. I will show it to you today," said Dorian, a strange smile on his handsome face.

Basil agreed to accompany him. He realised that it was late and this meant that he had already missed his train. He decided to take one the next day.

Chapter Thirteen

Murder

When they had reached the top of the house, Dorian asked Basil whether he really wanted to know everything about him.

"Yes, of course," said Basil.

"I will be delighted to give you all the answers. In fact, you are the person who deserves to know everything. You have played a very important role in my life," responded Dorian with a smile before taking his friend into the old schoolroom.

"Shut the door behind you Basil," Dorian said to the latter who had followed him upstairs. Dorian placed the lamp on the table and the room was bathed in some light. Dorian lit the half-burnt candle on the mantleshelf.

Basil noticed that the room was covered with dust. It did not have a lot of furniture. The carpet had holes in it and he even noticed a mouse run into a corner. The room had a damp smell that can usually be found in places which do not get much sunlight.

"Didn't you just say that only God can see our souls? Well, you can see mine if you draw back that curtain," said Dorian.

Basil could not understand the strange triumph in Dorian's voice. He hesitated.

"You won't do it, well then, I will do it for you," said Dorian and removed the curtain before the painting.

Basil gasped in horror. Staring back at him from the picture was the most horrible face. It seemed to be grinning at him. The artist was filled with disgust. But then he noticed that it was not altogether a horrible face. The thinning hair still showed a few golden strands. The eyes suddenly sparkled a beautiful blue. It was a picture of Dorian all right, but who had painted it, Basil asked himself. Almost immediately he recognised his own brush strokes. He held a candle to the corner of the frame and saw his own signature. Basil now recognised the picture as the one he had created. Why had it altered like this? How did it change into something so terrible?

Dorian had been watching Basil's reaction quietly. There was an expression of triumph in his eyes. Basil could not understand why.

He now asked his friend, "Do you remember how you praised my good looks? You and your friend together made me aware of the wonders of youth and beauty. Do you remember that I had made a wish?"

"Oh I remember that. But it is not possible... This room is damp... That is what must have affected the picture ... or the paint I had used was not right," Basil stammered desperately, trying to find an explanation to what was before his eyes.

"Can you see the man you idolised when you drew this picture?" asked Dorian bitterly.

"This is the face of the devil," responded Basil.

"This is the face of my soul," said Dorian, his voice expressing his helplessness.

"If this is true, what have you done with your life?" Basil exclaimed in horror before adding, "If this is true then you must be worse than what the people are saying about you." Saying this, Basil collapsed on the chair nearby.

Finally, he said, "Let us pray together, Dorian. The prayer of your pride has been answered. The prayer of your repentance will also be answered."

"It is too late Basil," Dorian sad emphatically.

"It is never too late. You have done enough evil in your life. My God! Don't you see the terrible thing leering at us," Basil pointed at the painting.

Dorian glanced at the portrait and suddenly felt a kind of terrible hatred for Basil. He continued to stare at the picture. It was as though the person in the picture was controlling him. Dorian looked around him. He noticed a knife on a small chest of drawers. He picked it up and walked up slowly

behind Basil. He struck the knife behind Basil's ear, crushing the man's head on the table and stabbing him again and again.

Dorian stepped back from Basil and waited, as if to let the reality of the deed set it. The room was completely quiet; just the sound of blood falling on the threadbare carpet.

Dorian was not horrified at what he had done. He had killed his friend. He felt strangely calm and went out to the balcony. He told himself that he had killed the man who had painted the fatal picture. Dorian went back to the room and looked at Basil's lifeless body. He did not feel any sadness or experience any guilt.

Back in his study after some time, Dorian was in a dilemma. He knew that he would have to face severe punishment if his crime was discovered. He hid Basil's coat and hat. He knew that Basil was a loner and therefore it would be quite some time before his acquaintances missed him. Furthermore, they all knew that he had left for Paris.

Dorian knew that the only person present in the house now was his valet. He decided to use him as his alibi. He put on his fur coat and hat and quietly stepped out of the front door. He then rang the bell. Around five minutes later, his valet opened the door. He had obviously been fast asleep.

"Sorry for waking you up. I forgot my keys at home," said Dorian as Francis closed the door after him. "Did anybody call for me?" Dorian asked innocently.

"Mr Hallward was here. He stayed till eleven and then left to catch his train for Paris. He said he would write to you," replied Francis.

"Ok, wake me up at nine tomorrow. I have some important work," said Dorian, his voice showing no emotion.

In his room, he couldn't sleep. He paced the floor for almost a quarter of an hour wondering what he would do with Basil's body. He finally came up with a plan. He decided he would put it into action the next day.

Chapter Fourteen

Alan Campbell

In spite of what he had done, Dorian slept peacefully through the night. As instructed, his valet woke him up with a glass of drinking chocolate at nine. Dorian greeted the warmth of the summer morning with a smile. But then the thought of Basil and the previous night came back to him. Basil's dead body had looked ugly in the darkness of the night. Dorian shuddered as he visualised how it would look in the light of the bright sun.

He decided not to think about it anymore. Or he would go mad.

At the breakfast table he concentrated on his

food and savoured every flavour. He finally decided to put his plan into action. He sat at his desk and wrote down two letters. He put one in his pocket and handed over the other to his valet. It was addressed to an Alan Campbell.

Alone in his study, Dorian spent quite some time reading. His thoughts would return to Basil sometimes. But he had now begun to see the situation in a detached way. He felt sympathy for the way Basil had to die. By now he had lost all feelings of guilt.

Dorian thought of Alan Campbell and wondered whether he would come in response to the letter. He remembered the time when he and Campbell had been the best of friends.

Alan Campbell and Dorian had been inseparable. They were seen together in various public functions. But now when the two came face-to-face, Dorian was the only one who smiled. Campbell had great interest in science. His interest and work in biology was often published in scientific papers. Dorian knew that only Campbell would be able to help him.

But would he come in response to the letter is what Dorian asked himself.

As he waited, a fear crept in his heart. What if Campbell refused to come? Finally, his valet came and announced that Mr Campbell had arrived.

"Thank you for coming Alan," said Dorian, his voice reflecting his relief.

"I promised myself that I would not enter your house ever again. But you said it was a matter of life and death," responded Campbell, his voice hard and cold.

"That is what it is," said Dorian calmly before adding, "In a room upstairs is a dead man. He has been dead for ten hours now. Don't ask me how he died, you have to do something for me…" said Dorian, when Campbell interrupted him with, "I don't want to know anything. I don't want to involve myself in your life. Keep your horrible secrets to yourself."

"You are the only one who can save me. You are a man of science. The man upstairs is supposed to be in Paris. Nobody will miss him for months. You have to get rid of the body for me.

You must change him and everything that belongs to him into a handful of ashes," said Dorian urgently.

"You are mad if you think I will help you. I don't care what happens to you. How dare you ask me to risk my reputation for you? I don't care what shame comes to you. Go to your friends. Don't come to me," fumed Campbell.

"I have killed the man upstairs. He is the one responsible for what I am today," Dorian finally confessed, a sadness in his voice.

"My God! Dorian you have murdered someone. But don't worry I will not tell this to anybody. It is not my business. But crime always catches up with the criminal. But I will not play any role in this. I absolutely refuse to do anything in the matter. It is insane of you to ask me," Campbell said bitterly.

Dorian now implored for his help. He reminded his old friend that this favour would be no more than a scientific experiment for him. He reminded him of the time when they

ALAN CAMPBELL

were good friends. But Campbell was adamant.
He ignored Dorian's pleas even when the latter
told him that if his crime was ever discovered
then he could be hanged.

Dorian realised that his pleas would not work
with his old friend. He took a piece of paper and
wrote something on it. He then pushed it across
the table towards Campbell and went on to stand
near the window.

Campbell's face went deathly pale as he read
the chit of paper. He could feel his heart beat
loudly in the hollow of his chest.

"I am sorry for this, Alan. But I have a letter
ready. I have to send it if you refuse to help me."
Dorian said calmly.

It was obvious that Dorian knew something
about Alan that the latter did not want to be
made public.

Campbell still looked horrified and his voice
quivered when he said, "I cannot help you."

"You don't have a choice. Don't delay this
now. Come upstairs," Dorian ordered his old
friend coolly.

"I will go home and get some things from my lab," Campbell finally said. He had realised that he had no choice but to give in to Dorian's blackmail. Dorian's reputation in the recent years convinced him that he was capable of living up to the threat he was making. Alan knew that he could not take a chance!

"You cannot leave the house. Make a note of what you want from your lab. My servant will take this to your assistant," Dorian said firmly, sounding more confident by the minute.

For the next 20 minutes the two men waited in Dorian's study. The only sound in the room was of the ticking clock. Campbell's hands were shivering from the time he had held Dorian's note. He suddenly looked up to his old friend's face. Dorian's eyes shimmered with unshed tears. There was sadness on that beautiful face. This was a sharp contrast to the fact that he was blackmailing his friend.

Finally the valet returned with the things. Dorian did not want his servant to be around in

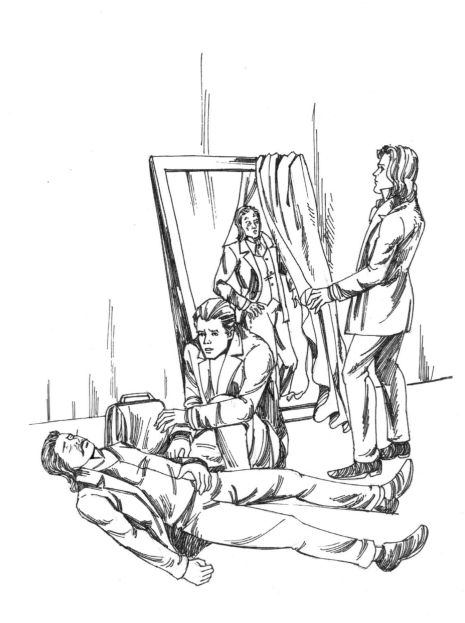

the house. So he sent him away for an errand that would take a few hours. Then he took Campbell upstairs, where the latter informed that his work would take around five hours. He did not need Dorian to be around during that time.

As the two men entered the room, Dorian's eyes fell on the portrait. He noticed that something red was glistening on one of his hands in the picture. It looked as though the picture had sweated blood. Dorian was horrified.

Campbell by now had started his work. He asked Dorian to leave the room. With one last look of disgust at Basil's lifeless body, Dorian left the room.

Darkness had fallen by the time Campbell came down to the study. Dorian was waiting for him.

"I have done my work. We do not have to see each other ever again," Campbell said sharply.

After he had left, Dorian went to the room upstairs. Basil's body was not there. But the room had a strong smell of nitric acid.

Chapter Fifteen

Evidence Removed

Dorian had a dinner invitation that day. Around 08:30 in the evening he arrived at Lady Narborough's house. He kept thinking about the day's events. But nobody looking at him could guess the riot of thoughts in his mind. He was calm as he spoke to his hostess and the others. Dorian himself was aware of how calm he looked and behaved. This double life he was living somehow strangely excited him.

It was a small party. Dorian did not find anybody interesting amongst the guests. He spent most part of the evening talking to his hostess. Lady Narborough was a widow who had two

daughters. They were now married and lived in the countryside. In fact, one of the daughters and her husband was visiting her now. This was the reason for the evening's little party. Time and again Dorian looked at the huge clock in the room. He wondered when he could leave.

But Dorian's bored expression changed suddenly as Lord Henry entered the party. He apologized for coming late. Dinner was soon served. Dorian did not have an appetite. His hostess mocked him for not doing justice to the food. Even Lord Henry remarked that something was different about him.

Lord Henry's dry wit soon had Dorian smiling. Lady Narborough joined in the conversation. The three discussed a common acquaintance and had a good laugh. The conversation steered to marriage and their hostess remarked that Dorian should get married. Lord Henry agreed with her, giving his own cynical views about marriage.

When Lady Narborough left the room, Lord Henry and Dorian got into a discussion about a party the latter was expected to host soon.

"By the way, Dorian, you left rather early yesterday. Where did you go? To the club?" asked Lord Henry suddenly.

"Yes ... I mean no. Not to the club, I walked around for quite some time ... I don't remember doing what ... I reached home at two ... You can ask my valet. I had forgotten my keys ... He opened the door for me," Dorian stammered through a reply, trying to sound convincing.

Lord Henry did not notice his anxiety. He asked Dorian whether they should go up to the drawing room. But Dorian wanted to go home and left soon after.

Back at home, he remembered the terror he had experienced at his friend's casual question. He did not want to experience that again. And for that, he had to take care of something important. He took Basil's coat and hat and burnt it in the fire. The smell of the burning things was very strong and it repelled Dorian. It took him over half an hour to completely burn down all signs that Basil had ever stepped into the house with

him that night. Now there was no evidence against him.

When he had finished his job, a strange madness struck him again. He took out the case of opium drug that he hid in his room. He looked at the clock. It was 20 minutes to midnight. He decided to go visit the opium dens of his city. He was not a stranger to the place. He slipped out of his house quietly and hired a carriage to take him to his destination.

Chapter Sixteen

James Meets Dorian

As the carriage went through the dark streets, it started raining. Dorian sat inside quietly. He could not get Basil out of his mind. He knew that he could not be forgiven for what he had done. But he wanted to forget everything. He cursed Basil for judging him and for making him angry. He was gradually becoming more restless. He desperately craved for opium. The darkness outside seemed to take everything in its arms. Everything around him looked ghostly and ugly.

Dorian finally reached his destination. He paid the driver and walked towards a shabby house. He knocked on the door in a particular way.

The interiors were as shabby as the outside. A sailor was sitting in the corner of the bar. His face covered with his arms. There were others in the room. Dorian ignored everything and walked towards the opium den. The first person Dorian saw there was Adrian Singleton. He remembered Basil's accusation of how he had ruined the man and caused him to leave the country. Adrian informed him that his brother had come to his rescue. Dorian was not interested in chatting with Adrian. He wanted to go somewhere, where nobody knew him.

As Dorian turned to leave, one woman tried to talk to him. He ignored her but gave her some money.

"There goes the devil's friend," said the woman in a hoarse voice.

"Don't call me that," responded Dorian in anger.

"Of Course! You want to be called Prince Charming. Isn't that right?" said the woman, her voice reflecting a strange bitterness.

The soldier who was sitting in the corner jumped to his feet. He looked around him frantically and then ran out of the door Dorian had walked out from.

Dorian in the meanwhile was walking rapidly through the rain outside. He was remembering Basil's words. Had he really ruined Adrian's life, he asked himself. But then he told himself that each man had his own destiny. He could not be held responsible for anybody.

Suddenly Dorian felt a hand catch him by the neck, from the back. He was flung against a wall. A hand closed around his neck. Dorian panicked and finally with some effort managed to wrench the tightening fingers away. Then he heard the click of a revolver. He realised that his attacker was holding a revolver at his head.

"Are you crazy? What have I done to you?" Dorian shouted.

"Keep quiet. If you stir I will shoot you. You have ruined the life of Sibyl Vane. She was my sister. She killed herself because of you. I have been looking for you for years. The two people who could have recognised you are both dead. I only knew your pet name. Today, I heard it by chance. Say your prayers. You are going to die today," said the sailor ferociously.

"I did not know her ... You are mad," stammered Dorian.

"Don't lie to me. I don't have much time. I board my ship today ... go down on your knees!" James Vane, the sailor, thundered in anger.

Dorian trembled with fear as he said "Stop. How long ago did your sister die?"

"Eighteen years. How do the years matter?" James asked incredulously.

There was now a note of triumph in Dorian's voice, "Eighteen years. Take me near a lamp and see my face."

As James saw Dorian's face in the light, he saw that the man could not be more than twenty. It was obvious to him that this was not the man his sister had loved. He pushed Dorian away, apologizing for his mistake.

"Oh My God! Oh My God! I could have murdered you!" he cried in horror.

Dorian pretended to be in a generous and forgiving mood. He asked James to keep the gun away or he would get into trouble.

"Forgive me, sir. I misunderstood. A chance word in the den put me on the wrong track." With this, apologizing profusely, he continued on his way.

"Why didn't you kill him?" James heard a woman's voice behind him. He realised that it was one of the women from the bar.

"He is not the man I was looking for. The man I am looking for must be around forty now. This one here is little more than a boy," answered James.

"Little more than a boy!" the woman laughed as she spat out the words, before adding, "Well, I have known Prince Charming for eighteen years."

James accused her of lying. But the woman said that she was saying the truth. She told James that this man was indeed the worst of the lot who

visited this place regularly. People believed that he had sold his soul to the devil. That is why he had remained young and handsome. The world around him had aged. James realised how he had been fooled. But it was too late now. The man responsible for his sister's death had disappeared into the darkness of the night.

Chapter Seventeen

He's Back

A week had gone by since the incident near the opium den. Dorian was entertaining some guests at his house in Selby. Lord Henry was also present. Like always, he was observing the people around him. He noticed Dorian in conversation with the Duchess of Monmouth. He decided to join in the discussion. Soon the three were talking about the virtues of beauty. The conversation soon steered towards love. Lord Henry, as usual, had his own cynical views about this emotion.

Dorian echoed the same opinion with, "Duchess, I always agree with Harry."

"Even when he is wrong?" asked the Duchess curiously.

"Harry is never wrong," replied Dorian confidently.

"And does his philosophy towards life make you happy?"

"I have never looked for happiness Duchess. I have only searched for pleasure ... and I have found that several times," responded Dorian with a mysterious smile.

The Duchess announced that she wanted to go and get dressed for the evening. Dorian offered to pluck some flowers for her. When he went away, Lord Henry playfully accused the Duchess of flirting with Dorian. He added that his friend had several admirers.

Suddenly, the two heard somebody groan. Then there was the sound of somebody falling. It came from the direction of the conservatory. The two ran towards the sound. To their horror, they discovered that Dorian was lying motionless on the floor. Some people carried him to the

drawing room of the house. Dorian had gained consciousness by then. But he was still trembling.

"What happened? ... Am I safe here?" he murmured anxiously.

"You just fainted, Dorian. You must be tired. Take some rest. You don't have to come for dinner," Lord Henry suggested.

"No, I will come down. I don't want to be alone," Dorian responded, struggling to stand steady on his feet.

Dorian went to his room. In some time he was at the dinner table with the guests. He was soon busy talking to his guests. But every few moments a terror ran through his body. He remembered the few moments before he had fainted. He had seen a man's face pressed against the window of the conservatory, where he was plucking the flowers. The man was watching him intently. It was James Vane.

Chapter Eighteen

The Stable

Dorian did not leave the house the next day. He lived in absolute terror, the movement of the curtains frightened him, the rustling of dry leaves outside rattled him. He kept remembering James Vane's face. He told himself that he was imagining things. Sybil Vane's brother had sailed away in his ship. He had not come back to kill him. But he could not suppress the terror in his heart. He told himself that he should not allow his mind to play these strange games with him. With his fear of James Vane, his memory of how he had murdered Basil also came back to haunt him. He imagined coming face-to-face with some

aspect of his crime all his life and shuddered at the thought.

Dorian dared to step out of the house only after another couple of days. He had told himself that living in such fear and helplessness was against his philosophy.

After breakfast he went for a walk with the Duchess. Later, he decided to join Sir Geoffrey. The Duchess's brother was out with a hunting party. The group had not had much luck with the sport. Suddenly they noticed a hare. Dorian begged Sir Geoffrey to not shoot the beautiful animal. But his companion ignored his sentimentality and shot at the hare. They heard the sound of a man in pain. Horrified, they realised that one of the servants must have been shot. There was much confusion after that, with people speculating about what must have happened. The hunting party dispersed soon after, disappointed that the sport ended this way.

Later, when Dorian was with Lord Henry he remarked that the incident was surely a bad

omen. His friend only laughed at this fear. But the feeling of terror that he had experienced for the past two days had returned.

"Can't you see a man among the trees, waiting for me?" Dorian pointed out anxiously.

"That is just your gardener, waiting to ask you what flowers should be put on the table tonight," Lord Henry corrected him.

Dorian told Henry that he wanted to go away, perhaps in a yacht, where he would be safe.

"Safe from what, Dorian? Are you in some trouble? Tell me about it. I will help you," Lord Henry offered.

Dorian said that there was nothing to tell. It was just his mind playing games with him. He just felt that something terrible was going to happen to him. Lord Henry just dismissed his crazy premonition. By then the Duchess had found them. But Dorian excused himself and went to his room for some rest.

Even as he lay on the sofa his mind was filled with terror. All he could think about was the servant who had been killed so carelessly.

In the evening, he called for his servant and asked him to pack his things. He did not want to stay here at Selby Royal anymore. He had every intention of catching the night train to London. Somehow he felt that this place was filled with bad omens. He wrote a note to Lord Henry asking him to take his place at the dinner.

Just as he was putting the note in the envelope, one of his servants arrived. Dorian realised that he must have come to talk about the servant who had been killed so unfortunately, to determine what compensation must be paid to the family.

"We don't know who he is sir," the servant informed Dorian.

"What do you mean? Was he not one of the servants?"

"No sir, we have never seen him before. He looked like a sailor," the servant offered.

Dorian's face lost all colour. He felt that his heart had stopped beating, "A sailor?" he repeated.

The servant informed him that the man who had been killed had tattoos on his arms. They had not found anything with him.

Dorian knew that the man must be James Vane. But he had to be sure. He demanded to see the body immediately. He accompanied the servant to the home farm where the body had been kept.

When Dorian reached the stable, it was dark. Only a single light flickered. He noticed that the body was lying on a pile of hay. Tha man's face was covered and he was wearing a coarse shirt and a pair of blue trousers. Dorian asked one of his men to uncover the face.

An involuntary cry of joy escaped Dorian's lips as he recognised the man to be James Vane. He stood looking at the dead man for some time. When he walked away, there were tears of relief in his eyes. He knew that he was safe at last.

Chapter Ninteen

Redemption

Several weeks had gone by since the episode at Dorian's estate. He had come to visit Lord Henry. Dorian was telling his friend that he had done too many dreadful things in his life. He now wanted to mend his ways. Lord Henry was quite amused by his decision.

Dorian told him that he had already started his reformation. It had happened quite recently. He had been visiting the countryside and staying at an inn. The innkeeper's daughter was quite enamoured by him. But he had decided not to encourage her attention. Lord Henry mocked

him that doing that must have given him a new thrill. He was so used to taking whatever took his fancy. Lord Henry added that the heartbroken girl would probably not be able to marry anybody else and remain unhappy all her life. So, indirectly, Dorian would be responsible for her unhappiness. Dorian dismissed his friend's suggestion.

The conversation soon steered to what everybody in London was speculating about — Basil Hallward's disappearance and Alan Campbell's suicide.

"Have you ever wondered that Basil might have been murdered?" Dorian offered, looking at his friend directly in order to see his reaction.

Lord Henry replied offhandedly, "That is not possible. Basil was too dull to have enemies. The only time I liked him was when he told me that he had become obsessed with you."

"What if I told you that I have murdered Basil?" Dorian said softly.

Lord Henry dismissed this suggestion. He said that Dorian was too polished to commit such a vulgar crime. He added that it was possible that Basil was dead, but his death must have occurred in a much less dramatic fashion.

Lord Henry suddenly asked Dorian about the portrait that Basil had painted. He remembered that Dorian had told him that the painting had been misplaced or stolen. Dorian immediately changed the topic.

"Tell me, Dorian, does it really benefit a man if he can gain everything in the world at the cost of his soul?" Lord Henry asked suddenly, causing Dorian's face to lose all colour.

Lord Henry explained that he had overheard a preacher asking this question to his audience.

Dorian philosophically responded that an individual's soul could be bought, sold or bartered away. His friend did not know the deeper meaning of Dorian's statement. Lord Henry was a man who lived by his wit and

humour. He did not want to dwell too long on these deep thoughts. He asked Dorian to play something cheerful on his piano.

"As you play, you must tell me how you have kept your youth," Lord Henry said jovially before adding, "You look like the same boy I had met so many years ago. You have experienced so many things in life. But they have not affected you. They have not spoilt you."

"I am not the same person Harry," said Dorian wistfully.

"Of course, you are. I wish I could change places with you," Lord Henry murmured.

"Do not say such things Harry. You do not know everything about me. If you did, you would turn away from me.

His friend laughed out aloud at this suggestion. He then suggested that Dorian accompany him to the club. But Dorian was in no mood to go out.

Just as Lord Henry was leaving, Dorian said, "Harry promise me that you will not lend the yellow book to anybody. It has spoiled me."

The older man could not detect the sadness in Dorian's voice. He mocked Dorian for having become moralistic. He even accused him of trying to deprive the world of the sins, actually pleasures, that he had become tired of. Before leaving, Lord Henry asked Dorian to be at the park the next morning at eleven.

Chapter Twenty

The Ugly Portrait

The night was warm as Dorian walked home. Two men walked past him. He overheard one of them whisper the name, Dorian Gray, to his companion. Dorian remembered the time when he enjoyed all this attention and importance. But he was tired of all this now. This is the reason why he went away from London so often. The little village he escaped to did not know that he was Dorian Gray. In fact, the girl that he was romantically involved with thought that he was a poor man. He had once told her that he was a wicked man, but she did not believe him. She only laughed.

He reached home to find his servants waiting for him. He sent them to bed and retired to the library. Alone in the library, he could not get the evening's conversation out of his mind. He had retained his youth. But did anyone know at what cost? He had corrupted his life in the worst way possible—that is, even though he had enjoyed every moment of it. He reminded himself that the people who had come to be associated with him had eventually been destroyed. He reminded himself that the portrait had faced the brunt of his corrupt life. His everlasting youth and good looks was just a mask over what he had become.

For a few brief moments Dorian felt intense regret at the way he had destroyed lives. Basil Hallward's murder, Alan Campbell's suicide and now James Vane's death—he had so much on his conscience. But the repentance did not last long. He told himself that he should not think of the past. What he should be thinking about now was the condition of his soul. Dorian decided that he wanted a new life. A life that was good.

227

He remembered the innkeeper's daughter, Hetty. Then he remembered the picture. Would it now reflect his goodness? Would the lines of evil on the face in the portrait disappear?

This thought gave rise to an overwhelming curiosity to see the portrait again. He took the lamp and slowly began to climb the stairs to the room upstairs, where the portrait rested. His footsteps echoed in the quiet empty house and there was a strange mixture of curiosity and fear in his heart.

In the empty dark room upstairs he lifted the screen over the picture and shuddered in horror. The picture was now uglier than it was before. The eyes in the picture reflected a cunningness that he had never seen before. He noticed that the red dew on the hand, which he had noticed right after he had killed Basil, was now brighter. It looked like fresh blood.

He remembered Lord Henry's words as he had told him about Hetty. He admitted the real reason why he had spared her. He acknowledged

that the reason was purely selfish. He knew that he could not be forgiven for most of his actions, most of his life. He just wanted to add this one good deed to his soul. And in doing so, he was only trying to save himself, not the girl. The "goodness" he had displayed was just a mask. He just wanted to find out how it would feel if he denied something to himself. He realised that Lord Henry's insinuations were completely true.

Dorian then noticed that the red on his hands in the portrait had become bigger. Did it mean that he would confess his crime, he asked himself. Would he be punished for Basil's murder? But where was the evidence against him? The only evidence was the picture.

In a moment of fury, Dorian decided that the picture must be destroyed. He had spent many sleepless nights thinking that the picture reflected the heinousness of his deeds. So in reality, the picture was the only evidence against him. He had been living in fear that somebody would see this picture. But he did not want

that anymore. He would destroy the picture, just as he had destroyed its creator. Once the picture was destroyed, he would be free of his past. Forever.

Looking around him, Dorian saw a knife. He realised it was the same knife that he had used to kill Basil. He had cleaned it thoroughly to remove all traces of blood. The knife now glistened like silver. It was the one he had used to kill Basil. He picked it up and stabbed the picture.

The servants in the house woke up to a loud cry, followed by a crash. People on the street also stopped to look at the great house. A couple of men walking nearby went ahead and returned with a policeman. They all looked at the house. It was in complete darkness. Only one light could be seen at a window on top of the house.

In the meanwhile, the servants could not understand anything. The valet, Francis, along with the coachman and the footman finally crept upstairs to the room on top of the house. There was no response as they knocked on the door.

Finally they climbed on the roof and came down on the balcony adjoining the room. They then forced open the old bolts of the window and entered the room.

When they entered the room, they saw a dazzling portrait of their master on the wall. It showed Dorian in all his beauty and youth. Lying on the floor was an old man in his evening dress, with a knife plunged in his chest. The man was withered, wrinkled and horrifyingly ugly. It was only when they noticed the rings on the man's fingers that they realised that it was their master, Dorian Gray.

About the Author

▪ Oscar Wilde

Oscar Wilde was born on 16 October 1854 in Dublin, Ireland. His father, William Wilde, was a famous doctor, but it was his mother, Jane Francesca Elgee, a poet, who had the most profound influence on Oscar Wilde's works.

An intelligent child, Oscar Wilde, fell in love with literature, especially Roman and Greek, at a very young age. He was one of the top students in school and went on to study, and excel academically at Trinity College, Dublin, and then at Oxford. It was at Oxford that Wilde first tried his hand at writing.

Wilde had his most creative years between 1885 and 1892. He wrote and published several essays, poems and plays during this time. In 1891, he published his first and only novel, The Picture of Dorian Gray.

Wilde's health suffered greatly during his last years and he died of meningitis on 30 November 1900 in Paris.

His writing is known for its wit, imagination and artistic mastery. Many of his famous plays, such as *The Importance of Being Earnest*, are still considered literary classics.

▪ Characters

Dorian Gray: The central character of the novel, Dorian Gray, is a vain and handsome man. He believes in enjoying life's pleasures, but his self-indulgent choices ultimately lead to his downfall.

Basil Howard: An artist, Basil Howard, is completely fascinated with Dorian Gray's beauty. It is under Dorian's patronage that Basil flourishes as an artist. Howard is the one who paints Dorian's portrait.

Lord Henry "Harry" Wotton: An aristocrat, Lord Wotton, is Basil's friend. He, too, is fascinated with Dorian Gray and his beauty. He is one who lures Dorian into living a self-indulgent existence. Unlike, Basil, Harry is completely amoral.

Sibyl Vane: A beautiful, young actress and Dorian Gray's love interest. Her love for Dorian has a negative influence on her talent as an actor. On learning that Dorian Gray doesn't love her, she commits suicide.

James Vane: Sibyl's brother, James Vane, is a sailor. He is very protective of his sister. James does not approve of Sibyl's relationship with Dorian Gray and blames him for Sibyl's suicide.

Alan Campbell: A one-time friend of Dorian Gray, Campbell cuts ties with Dorian and starts living an amoral and hedonistic life.

■ Questions

Chapter 1

- *What surprised Lord Henry about Basil's portrait?*
- *What is the real reason Basil would not exhibit Lord Henry's portrait?*

Chapter 2

- *What is Dorian Grey's wish regarding the portrait?*
- *Why does Dorian Grey not like the portrait?*

Chapter 3

- *What was the story of Dorian Gray's parentage?*
- *Why did Dorian want to leave with Henry after the party?*

Chapter 4

- *What does Lord Henry tell Dorian about marriage?*
- *What attracts Dorian to Sibyl?*

Chapter 5

- *What is the reason for Sibyl's happiness?*
- *How does Sibyl console James?*

Chapter 6

- *What is the news Lord Henry tells Basil?*
- *What happens after the play, between Dorian Grey and Sibyl?*

Chapter 7

- *How does Sibyl behave during the play?*
- *Why does Dorian break up with Sibyl?*

Chapter 8

- *How and why did Sibyl commit suicide?*
- *Why is Dorian shocked on the morning of Sibyl's death?*

Chapter 9

- *What shocks Basil about Dorian?*
- *How does Dorian prevent Basil from seeing the painting?*

Chapter 10

- *Where and why does Dorian hide the painting?*
- *What fascinates Dorian about the book Lord Henry lends him?*

Chapter 11

- *What was the most striking aspect about Dorian's looks, over the years?*
- *What are the two kinds of horrible changes which humans have to deal with?*

Chapter 12

- *What were the rumours doing the rounds regarding Dorian?*
- *What leads to the decision of Dorian to show Basil his painting?*

Chapter 13

- *How and why does Dorian kill Basil?*
- *How does Dorian use his valet as alibi?*

Chapter 14

- *How does Dorian trick Campbell into helping him?*
- *What is Campbell's reaction towards his friend?*

Chapter 15

- *What was the 'double life' that Dorian was leading?*
- *What strange things did Dorian do after Lady Narborough's party?*

Chapter 16

- *How does Dorian manage to free himself from James?*
- *Who tells James the truth about Dorian and how does this make James react?*

Chapter 17

- *What does Dorian say is his life's philosophy?*
- *Why does Dorian faint?*

Chapter 18

- *What happens at the hunting party?*
- *What is the true identity of the 'servant' killed during the shooting? What is Dorian's reaction?*

Chapter 19

- *What secret does Dorian reveal to Lord Henry?*
- *What does Lord Henry envy about Dorian?*

Chapter 20

- *What does Dorian notice about the portrait?*
- *How does Dorian die? What happens to the painting and why?*